To Constance

ILLUSTRATED BY FELIKS TOPOLSKI

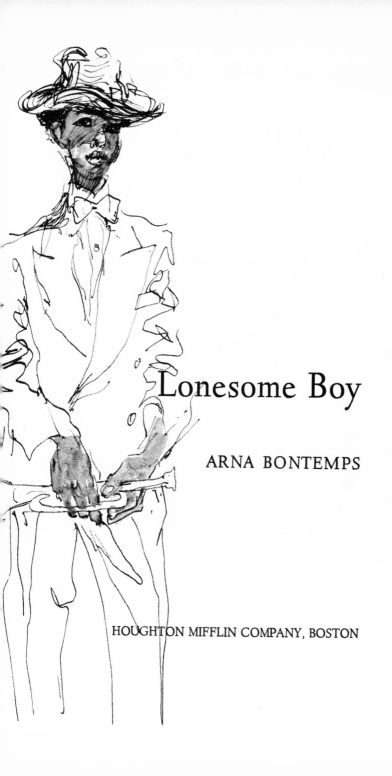

Lonesome Boy

ARNA BONTEMPS

HOUGHTON MIFFLIN COMPANY, BOSTON

LONESOME BOY

WHEN BUBBER first learned to play the trumpet, his old grandpa winked his eye and laughed.

"You better mind how you blow that horn, sonny boy. You better mind."

"I like to blow loud, I like to blow fast, and I like to blow high," Bubber answered. "Listen to this, Grandpa." And he went on blowing with his eyes closed.

When Bubber was a little bigger, he began carrying his trumpet around with him wherever he went, so his old grandpa scratched his whiskers, took the corncob pipe out of his mouth, and laughed again.

"You better mind where you blow that horn, boy," he warned. "I used to blow one myself, and I know."

Bubber smiled. "Where did you ever blow music, Grandpa?"

2

"Down in New Orleans and all up and down the river. I blowed trumpet most everywhere in my young days, and I tell you, you better mind where you go blowing."

"I like to blow my trumpet in the school band when it marches, I like to blow it on the landing when the river boats come in sight, and I like to blow it among the trees in the swamp," he said, still smiling. But when he looked at his grandpa again, he saw a worried look on the old man's face, and he asked, "What's the matter, Grandpa, ain't that all right?"

Grandpa shook his head. "I wouldn't do it if I was you."

That sounded funny to Bubber, but he was not in the habit of disputing his grandfather. Instead he said, "I don't believe I ever heard you blow the trumpet, Grandpa. Don't you want to try blowing on mine now?"

Again the old man shook his head. "My blowing days are long gone," he said. "I still got the lip, but I ain't got the teeth. It takes good teeth to blow high notes on a horn, and these I got ain't much good. They're store teeth."

That made Bubber feel sorry for his grandfather, so he whispered softly, "I'll mind where I blow my horn, Grandpa."

He didn't really mean it though. He just said it to make his grandpa feel good. And the very next day he was half a mile out in the country blowing his horn in a cornfield. Two or three evenings later he was blowing it on a shady lane when the sun went down and not paying much attention where he went.

When he came home, his grandpa met him. "I heard you blowing your horn a long ways away," he said. "The air was still. I could hear it easy."

"How did it sound, Grandpa?"

"Oh, it sounded right pretty." He paused a moment, knocking the ashes out of his pipe, before adding, "Sounded like you mighta been lost."

That made Bubber ashamed of himself, because he knew he had not kept his word and that he was not minding where he blew his trumpet. "I know what you mean, Grandpa," he answered. "But I can't do like you say. When I'm blowing my horn, I don't always look where I'm going."

Grandpa walked to the window and looked out. While he was standing there, he hitched his overalls up a little higher. He took a red handkerchief from his pocket and wiped his forehead. "Sounded to me like you might have been past Barbin's Landing."

"I was lost," Bubber admitted.

"You can end up in some funny places when you're just blowing a horn and not paying attention. I know," Grandpa insisted. "I know."

"Well, what do you want me to do, Grandpa?"

The old man struck a kitchen match on the seat of his pants and lit a kerosene lamp, because the room was black dark by now. While the match was still burning, he lit his pipe. Then he sat down and stretched out his feet. Bubber was on a stool on the other side of the room, his trumpet under his arm. "When you go to school and play your horn in the band, that's all right," the old man said. "When you come home, you ought to put it in the case and leave it there. It ain't good to go traipsing around with a horn in your hand. You might get into devilment."

"But I feel lonesome without my trumpet, Grandpa," Bubber pleaded. "I don't like to go around without it any time. I feel lost."

Grandpa sighed. "Well, there you are—lost with it and lost without it. I don't know what's going to become of you, sonny boy."

"You don't understand, Grandpa. You don't understand."

The old man smoked his pipe quietly for a few minutes and then went off to bed, but Bubber did not move. Later on, however, when he heard his grandpa

7

snoring in the next room, he went outdoors, down the path and around the smokehouse, and sat on a log. The night was still. He couldn't hear anything louder than a cricket. Soon he began wondering how his trumpet would sound on such a still night, back there behind the old smokehouse, so he put the mouthpiece to his lips very lightly and blew a few silvery notes. Immediately Bubber felt better. Now he knew for sure that Grandpa didn't understand how it was with a boy and a horn— a lonesome boy with a silver trumpet. Bubber lifted his horn toward the stars and let the music pour out.

Presently a big orange moon rose, and everything Bubber could see changed suddenly. The moon was so big it made the smokehouse and the trees and the fences seem small. Bubber blew his trumpet loud, he blew it fast, and he blew it high, and in just a few minutes he forgot all about Grandpa sleeping in the house.

He was afraid to talk to Grandpa after that. He was afraid Grandpa might scold him or warn him or try in some other way to persuade him to leave his trumpet in its case. Bubber was growing fast now. He knew what he liked, and he did not think he needed any advice from Grandpa.

Still, he loved his grandfather very much, and he had no intention of saying anything that would hurt him. Instead he decided to leave home. He did not tell Grandpa what he was going to do. He just waited till the old man went to sleep in his bed one night. Then he quietly blew out the lamp, put his trumpet under his arm and started walking down the road from Marksville to Barbin's Landing.

No boat was there, but Bubber did not mind. He knew one would come by before morning, and he knew that he would not be lonesome so long as he had his trumpet with him. He found a place on the little dock where he could lean back against a post and swing his feet over the edge while playing, and the time passed swiftly. And when he finally went aboard a river boat, just before morning, he found a place on the deck that suited him just as well and went right on blowing his horn.

Nobody asked him to pay any fare. The river boat men did not seem to expect it of a boy who blew a trumpet the way Bubber did. And in New Orleans the cooks in the kitchens where he ate and the people who kept the rooming houses where he slept did not seem to expect him to pay either. In fact, people seemed to think that a boy who played a trumpet where the patrons of a restaurant could hear him or for the guests of a rooming house should receive money for it. They began to throw money around Bubber's feet as he played his horn.

At first he was surprised. Later he decided it only showed how wrong Grandpa had been about horn blowing. So he picked up all the money they threw, bought himself fancy new clothes and began looking for new places to play. He ran into boys who played guitars or bullfiddles or drums or other instruments, and he played right along with them. He went out with them to play for picnics or barbecues or boat excursions or dances. He played early in the morning and he played late at night, and he bought new clothes and dressed up so fine he scarcely knew himself in a mirror. He scarcely knew day from night.

It was wonderful to play the trumpet like that, Bubber thought, and to make all that money. People telephoned to the rooming house where he lived and asked for him nearly every day. Some sent notes asking if he would play his trumpet at their parties. Occasion-

10

ally one would send an automobile to bring him to the place. Bubber liked riding through the pretty part of the city to the ballrooms in which well-dressed people waited to dance to his music. He enjoyed even more the times when he was taken to big white-columned houses in the country, houses surrounded by old trees with moss on them.

But he went to so many places to play his trumpet, he forgot where he had been and he got into the habit of not paying much attention. That was how it was the day he received a strange call on the telephone. A voice that sounded like a very proper gentleman said, "I would like to speak to the boy from Marksville, the one who plays the trumpet."

"I'm Bubber, sir. I'm the one."

"Well, Bubber, I'm having a very special party tonight—very special," the voice said. "I want you to play for us."

Bubber felt a little drowsy because he had been sleeping when the phone rang,

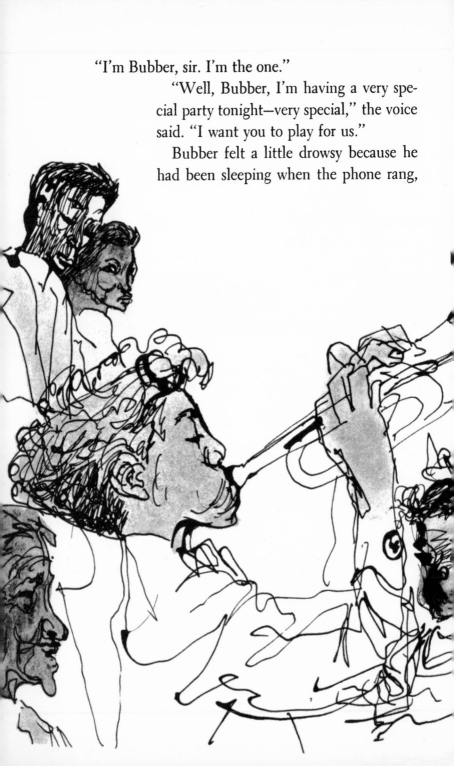

and he still wasn't too well awake. He yawned as he answered, "Just me, sir? You want me to play by myself?"

"There will be other musicians, Bubber. You'll play in the band. We'll be looking for you."

"Where do you live, sir?" Bubber asked sleepily.

"Never mind about that, Bubber, I'll send my chauffeur with my car. He'll bring you."

The voice was growing faint by this time, and Bubber was not sure he caught the last words. "Where did you say, sir?" he asked suddenly. "When is it you want me?"

"I'll send my chauffeur," the voice repeated and then faded out completely.

Bubber put the phone down and went back to his bed to sleep some more. He had played his trumpet very late the night before, and now he just couldn't keep his eyes open.

Something was ringing when he woke up again. Was it the telephone? Bubber jumped out of bed and ran to answer, but the phone buzzed when he put it to his ear. There was nobody on the line. Then he knew it must have been the doorbell. A moment later he heard the door open, and footsteps came down the dark hall toward his room. Before Bubber could turn on the light, the footsteps were just outside his room, and a man's voice said, "I'm the chauffeur. I've brought the car to take you to the dance."

"So soon?" Bubber asked, surprised.

The man laughed. "You must have slept all day. It's night now, and we have a long way to drive."

"I'll put on my clothes," Bubber said.

The street light was shining through the window,

so he did not bother to switch on the light in his room. Bubber never liked to open his eyes with a bright light shining, and anyway he knew right where to put his hands on the clothes he needed. As he began slipping into them, the chauffeur turned away. "I'll wait for you on the curb," he said.

"All right," Bubber called. "I'll hurry."

When he finished dressing, Bubber took his trumpet off the shelf, closed the door of his room, and went out to where the tall chauffeur was standing beside a long, shiny automobile. The chauffeur saw him coming and opened the door to the back seat. When Bubber stepped in, he threw a lap robe across his knees and closed the door. Then the chauffeur went around to his place in the front seat, stepped on the starter, switched on his headlights, and sped away.

The car was finer than any Bubber had ridden in before, and the motor purred so softly, the chauffeur drove it so smoothly, Bubber soon began to feel sleepy again. One thing puzzled him, however. He had not yet seen the chauffeur's face, and he wondered what the man looked like. But now the chauffeur's cap was down so far over his eyes and his coat collar was turned up so high Bubber could not see his face at all, no matter how far he leaned forward.

After a while he decided it was no use. He would have to wait till he got out of the car to look at the man's face. In the meantime he would sleep. Bubber pulled the lap robe up over his shoulders, stretched out on the wide back seat of the car and went to sleep again.

The car came to a stop, but Bubber did not wake up till the chauffeur opened the door and touched his shoulder. When he stepped out of the car, he could see nothing but dark, twisted trees with moss hanging from them. It was a dark and lonely place, and Bubber was so surprised he did not remember to look at the chauffeur's face. Instead, he followed the tall figure up a path covered with leaves to a white-columned house with lights shining in the windows.

Bubber felt a little better when he saw the big house with the bright windows. He had played in such houses before, and he was glad for a chance to play in another. He took his trumpet from under his arm, put the mouthpiece to his lips and blew a few bright, clear notes as he walked. The chauffeur did not turn around. He led Bubber to a side entrance, opened the door and pointed the boy to the room where the dancing had already started. Without ever showing his face, the chauffeur closed the door and returned to the car.

Nobody had to tell Bubber what to do now. He found a place next to the big fiddle that made the rhythms, waited a moment for the beat, then came in with his trumpet. With the bass fiddle, the drums, and the other stringed instruments backing him up, Bubber began to bear down on his trumpet. This was just what he liked. He played loud, he played fast, he played high, and it was all he could do to keep from laughing when he thought about Grandpa and remembered how the old man had told him to mind how he played his horn. Grandpa should see him now, Bubber thought.

Bubber looked at the dancers swirling on the ballroom floor under the high swinging chandelier, and he wished that Grandpa could somehow be at the window and see how they glided and spun around to the music of his horn. He wished the old man could get at least one glimpse of the handsome dancers, the beautiful women in bright-colored silks, the slender men in black evening clothes.

As the evening went on, more people came and began dancing. The floor became more and more crowded, and Bubber played louder and louder, faster and faster, and by midnight the gay ballroom seemed to be spinning like a pinwheel. The floor looked like glass under the dancers' feet. The draperies on the windows were like gold, and Bubber was playing his trumpet so hard and so fast his eyes looked ready to pop out of his head.

But he was not tired. He felt as if he could go on playing like this forever. He did not even need a short rest. When the other musicians called for a break and went outside to catch a breath of fresh air, he kept right on blowing his horn, running up the scale and down, hitting high C's, swelling out on the notes and then letting them fade away. He kept the dancers

entertained till the full band came back, and he blew the notes that started them to dancing again.

Bubber gave no thought to the time, and when a breeze began blowing through the tall windows, he paid no attention. He played as loud as ever, and the dancers whirled just as fast. But there was one thing that did bother him a little. The faces of the dancers began to look thin and hollow as the breeze brought streaks of morning mist into the room. What was the matter with them? Were they tired from dancing all night? Bubber wondered.

But the morning breeze blew stronger and stronger. The curtains flapped, and a gray light appeared in the windows. By this time Bubber noticed that the people who were dancing had no faces at all, and though they continued to dance wildly as he played his trumpet, they seemed dim and far away. Were they disappearing?

Soon Bubber could scarcely see them at all. Suddenly he wondered where the party had gone. The musicians too grew dim and finally disappeared. Even the room with the big chandelier and the golden draperies at the windows was fading away like a dream. Bubber was frightened when he realized that nothing was left, and he was alone. Yes, definitely, he was alone, but— but *where*? Where was he now?

He never stopped blowing his shiny trumpet. In fact, as the party began to break up in this strange way, he blew harder than ever to help himself feel brave again.

He also closed his eyes. That is how he happened to notice how uncomfortable the place where he was sitting had become. It was about as unpleasant as sitting on a log. And it was while his eyes were closed that he first became aware of leaves near by, leaves rustling and blowing in the cool breeze.

But he could not keep his eyes closed for long with so much happening. Bubber just had to peep eventually, and when he did, he saw only leaves around him. Certainly leaves were nothing to be afraid of, he thought, but it was a little hard to understand how the house and room in which he had been playing for the party all night had been replaced by branches and leaves like this. Bubber opened both his eyes wide, stopped blowing his horn for a moment and took a good, careful look at his surroundings.

Only then did he discover for sure that he was not in a house at all. There were no dancers, no musicians, nobody at all with him, and what had seemed like a rather uncomfortable chair or log was a large branch. Bubber was sitting in a pecan tree, and now he realized that this was where he had been blowing his trumpet so fast and so loud and so high all night. It was very discouraging.

But where was the chauffeur who had brought him here and what had become of the party and the graceful dancers? Bubber climbed down and began looking around. He could see no trace of the things that had

seemed so real last night, so he decided he had better go home. Not home to the rooming house where he slept while in New Orleans, but home to the country where Grandpa lived.

He carried his horn under his arm, but he did not play a note on the bus that took him back to Marksville next day. And when he got off the bus and started walking down the road to Grandpa's house in the country, he still didn't feel much like playing anything on his trumpet.

Grandpa was sleeping in a hammock under a china-berry tree when he arrived, but he slept with one eye open, so Bubber did not have to wake him up. He just stood there, and Grandpa smiled.

"I looked for you to come home before now," the old man said.

"I should have come sooner, Grandpa," Bubber answered, shamefaced.

"I expected you to be blowing on your horn when you came."

"That's what I want to talk to you about, Grandpa."

The old man sat up in the hammock and put his feet on the ground. He scratched his head and reached for his hat. "Don't tell me anything startling," he said. "I just woke up, and I don't want to be surprised so soon."

Bubber thought maybe he should not mention what had happened. "All right, Grandpa," he whispered,

looking rather sad. He leaned against the chinaberry tree, holding the trumpet under his arm, and waited for Grandpa to speak again.

Suddenly the old man blinked his eyes as if remembering something he had almost forgotten. "Did you mind how you blew on that horn down in New Orleans?" he asked.

"Sometimes I did. Sometimes I *didn't*," Bubber confessed.

Grandpa looked hurt. "I hate to hear that, sonny boy," he said. "Have you been playing your horn at barbecues and boatrides and dances and all such as that?"

"Yes, Grandpa," Bubber said, looking at the ground.

"Keep on like that and you're apt to wind up playing for a devil's ball."

Bubber nodded sadly. "Yes, I know."

Suddenly the old man stood up and put his hand on Bubber's shoulder. "Did a educated gentleman call you on the telephone?"

"He talked so proper I could hardly make out what he was saying."

"Did the chauffeur come in a long shiny car?"

Bubber nodded again. "How did you know about all that, Grandpa?"

"Didn't I tell you I used to blow music, sonny boy?" Grandpa closed his eyes a moment. When he opened them again, he shook his head slowly. "Any time a boy with a trumpet takes off for New Orleans without telling anybody good-bye—well, sooner or later, one way or another, he's apt to hear from strange people."

"I should have hung up the telephone," Bubber mumbled, feeling ashamed of himself.

Suddenly Grandpa's voice grew stern. "You should have minded what I told you at the first. Blow your horn when you're a-mind to, but put it down when you're through. When you go traipsing through the woods, leave it on the shelf. When you feel lonesome, don't touch it. A horn can't do nothing for lonesomeness but make it hurt worse. When you're lonesome, that's the time to go out and find somebody to talk to. Come back to your trumpet when the house is full of company or when people's passing on the street. That's what I tried to tell you before."

"I'm going to mind you this time, Grandpa," Bubber promised. "I'm going to mind every word you say."

Grandpa laughed through his whiskers. "Well, take your trumpet in the house and put it on the shelf while I get you something to eat," he said. "Raising up a boy like you ain't easy. First you tell him when to pick up his horn, then you tell him when to put it down. Some things he just has to learn for himself, I reckon."

Bubber smiled too. He was hungry, and he had not tasted any of Grandpa's cooking for a long time.